A Bus of Our Own

WRITTEN BY Freddi Williams Evans

ILLUSTRATED BY Shawn Costello

Albert Whitman & Company

Morton Grove, Illinois

To my uncles, the late C.W. "Smith" Cotten and Joe E. Cotten, Sr.;
my cousins, Carrie Bell Lewis and Mable Lewis Seaton; the people
who rode in or contributed to the first bus; Coleen Salley;
and Patricia McKissack. —F. W. E.

To my son, Drew Costello. —S. C.

Special thanks to my faithful friend Patricia Mack Preston and her family. Also thanks to Marcellus Preston,
Charles Mack and his sons, Roniece King, and members of the Union Street Church. Thanks to Ciarra Phillip
and to the children of Hollifield Station Elementary School, and to Cynthia Crowder. Thanks to Judy Fulmer
for her color critiques, and to my coach, Ann Harding. Thanks also to my friends near and far, and to my
prayer buddy, Eileen Clark, who helped me through, and to the good Lord for His faithfulness. —S. C.

*

Library of Congress Cataloging-in-Publication Data
Evans, Freddi Williams.
A bus of our own / written by Freddi Williams Evans ; illustrated by Shawn Costello.
p. cm.
Summary: Although she really wants to go to school, walking the five miles is very difficult
for Mable Jean and the other black children, so she tries to find a way to get a bus
for them like the white children have. Based on real events in Mississippi.
ISBN 0-8075-0970-1 (hardcover)
ISBN 0-8075-0971-X (paperback)
1. African Americans — Juvenile fiction. [1. African Americans — Fiction.
2. Schools — Fiction. 3. School buses — Fiction.
4. Segregation — Fiction.] I. Costello, Shawn, ill. II. Title.
PZ7.E8853 Bu 2001 [E] — dc21 2001000888

The paintings are rendered in oil on paper.
The design is by Scott Piehl.

YOU GOT TO KEEP UP, MABLE JEAN," Jeff insisted.
Mable Jean tried to make her feet move faster. But
she just couldn't. Now she and her big brother were
way behind the other children.

"I'm not gonna carry you," he said. "If you can't keep up,
you'll have to stay home from school."

"I'll keep up," she mumbled.

Jeff was reminding Mable Jean of what their papa had told her. "If you can't walk the five miles, you'll have to stay home till next year." But Mable Jean's mind <u>was</u> <u>set on</u> going to school that year, and nothing was going to stop her.

By the time Jeff took Mable Jean to her classroom, school had already started. "Get a drink of water from <u>the cistern</u> and rest awhile," her teacher, Miz Powell, told her.

Mable Jean joined the class when it was time to count chinaberries. She counted all the way to fifteen. "Very good, Mable Jean," Miz Powell said. "Now help your neighbor."

After school, Mable Jean and the other children walked home along the gravel road. "Go ahead," Jeff told his friends. "I have to walk with Mable Jean." Cars passed them. Then a school bus passed. But it only carried white children.

"Na-na-na-na-na, you got to wa-alk," they teased, and called Mable Jean and the others names. Jeff held her hand so she wouldn't be too afraid.

They took a short cut through the Henderson place. But suddenly Mable Jean stepped hard on the edge of a stump. Pain shot through her foot and up her leg like a hundred bumblebees had stung her. Then her knees buckled and she landed on the ground.

"Come on, Mable Jean!" Jeff said as he stopped to help.

"I'll ... I'll walk," she insisted. But she couldn't even stand up. Jeff said he wasn't going to carry her, but he did.

Mable Jean's heart hurt worse than her foot when she remembered her papa's warning.

"If you stay off of your foot, it'll get better sooner," her mama said when she put her in bed. Mable Jean still worried about what her papa would say.

"Looks like the walk is too much, Mable Jean," he said when he came in from the field.

"Papa, please don't make me stay home till next year," she pleaded. "Hurting my foot was an accident. I can make the walk fine. *Please* give me another chance."

He dropped his head, and everyone was silent.

"Well ..." he hesitated. "Well ... we'll try it again."

"Thank you, Papa," she said, and slid under the covers before he changed his mind.

On Mable Jean's first day back in school, it rained. When the school bus passed, muddy water splashed all over Mable Jean and Jeff. Water got in her boots, and her feet slipped and rubbed so much that they <u>blistered</u>.

"Next time, when your feet get wet, take your boots off," her mama told her. "<u>This Epsom salt</u> water will help your feet along. But the way they look, you gonna have to stay home for a while."

"Stay home!" Mable Jean cried. "I want to go to school! Why can't we ride a school bus like the white children, anyway?"

"Now, Mable Jean," her papa answered. "You know the folks who run <u>the county</u> don't give us folks no school buses."

"Can you ask somebody to give us a bus, Papa?" Mable Jean said.

He put his arms around her. "It's not that easy, Mable Jean. I want a bus, too, but I don't know who to ask."

That evening, Mable Jean heard her parents talk about the bus. Her papa said, "You know, we don't own this place. If we make trouble, we could get kicked off the land."

11

"We missed you," Miz Powell said when Mable Jean returned. "We're glad you're back."

"I'm glad I'm back, too," she replied. "I like school, but I'll have to stop again soon — 'cause of the weather this time."

"Me, too," Henry said. "My mama said I could catch my <u>death of cold</u> walking to school when it's cold and rainy."

"I saw <u>frost</u> on the ground this morning," Sam added.

"Can you ask somebody to give us a bus, Miz Powell?" Mable Jean asked. "If we had a bus to ride, we wouldn't have to stop coming to school."

"The only people I know to ask are the ones who run the county," she answered. "Your parents should ask them." When Miz Powell said that, Mable Jean remembered what she had heard her papa say. She knew he would not want to make trouble.

13

That afternoon as Mable Jean and Jeff walked home from school, a fancy black car stopped beside them. "Jeff," the driver called, "Get in. I'll give you and Lil' Mable a ride."

It was their Cousin Smith, and he was on his way home from town. He owned lots of land and hired people to work for him. Sometimes Jeff and other children earned money picking cotton for him.

Mable Jean slid into the back seat. Then Jeff got in after her. She had never ridden in such a fancy car before. She knew that it had to cost a lot of money. If Cousin Smith had enough money to buy a car like that, then maybe ...

"Cousin Smith," she called as the car stopped.

"What you want, Lil' Mable?" he asked.

"Well ..." she hesitated. "Can you get a bus for us? Me and my friends have to stop school soon 'cause of the weather. We don't want to stop. If we had a bus, we wouldn't have to, and I wouldn't keep hurting my feet like I do."

"A bus? I want to help, Lil' Mable, but I don't know anything about buses."

14

Mable Jean prayed that Cousin Smith would find out something about buses, and before long, he did. When she saw his car pull into her yard the next week, she <u>crossed her fingers</u> and dashed outside.

"Last week, Lil' Mable Jean asked if I could get a school bus," he told her parents. "I've been figuring on it and decided to buy a bus if enough parents support me. They will have to pay for the children to ride. Now, I know we're already paying <u>taxes</u>, and rightly, we should have a bus. It looks like we have to pay twice for our children to get a good learning."

"I'll see what folks say," Mable Jean's mama said.

17

The next Sunday, she made an announcement in church. "Our own Brother Smith's got a plan to get a school bus for our children," she said. "But we'll have to support him. We'll have to pay extra for the children to ride. All y'all that's willing and able, meet me under the tree after service."

18

"Our children need an education in order to get ahead. But they can't get an education if they can't get to school," she told the crowd after church.

"I'll be willing to take on another ironing job," Miz McDonald said.

"I can pick cotton after school," said Henry's older brother.

"I can take on an extra <u>wash job</u>," Miz Rouser said.

Other parents also agreed to pay for their children to ride the bus. "It looks like we have the start we need," Mable Jean's mama said.

Cousin Smith went on with his plan. He purchased an old bus that was once used by the white school. But it was in such bad shape that it stopped before he made it home. "Don't look like this is gonna do," Mable Jean's papa said as he hitched it to a tractor.

"Yeah, but sometimes it takes two to make one,"
Cousin Smith replied.

"Two to make one?" Mable Jean thought. Then she
remembered how her grandmother used two flour <u>sacks</u>
to make one slip.

"Cousin Smith bought a bus, all right," Mable Jean complained to her friends. "It's so old it doesn't even run. My papa is gonna help work on it next Saturday. But if they can't fix it, we'll still have to walk."

"My papa can fix cars. I'll ask him to fix the bus," Sam said.

"I'll ask my daddy to help," Henry added.

When they got to Cousin Smith's house that Saturday, there was a surprise. Instead of one, there were two old buses!

Then with everyone's help, the best parts of the two buses
were put together to make one good bus.

"Let me take a look at the engine," Sam's papa said.

"I'll fix the tires," said Henry's daddy.

"I brought this wood for the floor," said Louise's daddy.

Mable Jean's papa and brother made two long benches. "I want to help, too," Mable Jean said.

"You can help paint," her papa told her. When the benches were dry, they put one under each row of windows, and the inside of the bus was ready. Soon the outside was ready, too.

27

Mable Jean and Jeff stood at their bus stop bright and early that first morning. Family, friends, and neighbors stood with them.

"Here it comes!" Mable Jean shouted. They all clapped and waved as the bus <u>approached</u>.

28

"Thank you for getting a bus for us, Cousin Smith," Mable Jean said as she hurried <u>aboard</u>. Then she gave him five cents and sat on the bench right behind him.

People cheered as the bus pulled away. They had come out to see the <u>colored</u> children ride a bus of their own.

Everyone agreed it was a sight worth paying twice to see.

Author's Note

Based on real events, *A Bus of Our Own* depicts the spirit of African-Americans who lived in the rural Ridley Hill Baptist Church Community of Madison, Mississippi, after World War II and before the civil rights era. Although African-American citizens paid taxes and many of them owned land, they received "separate and unequal" public services such as schools and school transportation.

Like Mable Jean's family, most African-Americans who did not own land were victims of sharecropping, a system under which they lived on and worked the land for a share of the crop but received little or no money as payment for their labor. This arrangement kept the sharecroppers in debt to landowners and in a state of quasi-slavery.

In 1949, with the leadership of Mrs. Carrie Bell Lewis, whose daughter Mable Maxine is the "Mable Jean" of this story, and with active support from other parents, Clifton W. "Smith" Cotten purchased and operated the first school bus for their children.

Spurred on by community efforts, in 1950 the Madison County School Board offered Mr. Cotten a contract to provide two buses and receive $120 a month for each. His younger brother, Joe E. Cotten, Sr., purchased and operated the second bus. In 1954, the county provided buses for its African-American children and hired drivers. This was the same year as the landmark *Brown v. Board of Education* case in which the United States Supreme Court ruled unanimously that racially segregated schools deprive minorities of equal educational opportunities and are unconstitutional.

Mable Maxine Lewis (later Seaton) completed eighth grade at the local school and high school at Tougaloo Preparatory School in Tougaloo, Mississippi. She earned a B.A. degree in Elementary Education at Tougaloo College in 1968.